AF236785

Thomas Gray

An Elegy Written in a Country Churchyard

SALZWASSER
VERLAG

Thomas Gray

An Elegy Written in a Country Churchyard

1st Edition | ISBN: 978-3-75250-338-8

Place of Publication: Frankfurt am Main, Germany

Year of Publication: 2020

Salzwasser Verlag GmbH, Germany.

Reprint of the original, first published in 1869.

An Elegy

WRITTEN IN A COUNTRY CHURCHYARD

BY THOMAS GRAY

London:

SAMPSON LOW, SON, AND MARSTON

CROWN BUILDINGS, FLEET STREET

1869

The curfew tolls the knell of parting day.

List of Illustrations

From Drawings by R. BARNES, R. P. LEITCH, E. M. WIMPERIS, *and others.*

PRINTED IN COLOURS BY COOPER, CLAY, & CO.

The lowing herd winds slowly o'er the lea.

AN Elegy

HE curfew tolls the knell of parting day,
　The lowing herd winds slowly o'er the lea,
The ploughman homeward plods his weary way,
　And leaves the world to darkness and to me.

Now fades the glimmering landscape on the sight,
　And all the air a solemn stillness holds,
Save where the beetle wheels his droning flight,
　And drowsy tinklings lull the distant folds:

The cock's shrill clarion.

Save that from yonder ivy-mantled tower,

    The moping owl does to the moon complain

Of such as, wandering near her secret bower,

    Molest her ancient solitary reign.

Beneath those rugged elms, that yew tree's shade,

    Where heaves the turf in many a mould'ring heap,

Each in his narrow cell for ever laid,

    The rude forefathers of the hamlet sleep.

The breezy call of incense-breathing morn,

    The swallow twitt'ring from the straw-built shed,

The cock's shrill clarion, or the echoing horn,

    No more shall rouse them from their lowly bed.

Climb his knees the envied kiss to share.

.

Oft did the harvest to their sickle yield.

Homely joys.

For them no more the blazing hearth shall burn,
　Or busy housewife ply her evening care;
No children run to lisp their sire's return,
　Or climb his knees the envied kiss to share.

Oft did the harvest to their sickle yield,
　Their furrow oft the stubborn glebe has broke:
How jocund did they drive their team afield!
　How bow'd the woods beneath their sturdy stroke!

Let not ambition mock their useful toil,
　Their homely joys, and destiny obscure;
Nor grandeur hear with a disdainful smile
　The short and simple annals of the poor.

The paths of glory lead but to the grave.

The long-drawn aisle, and fretted vault.

The boast of heraldry, the pomp of power,
    And all that beauty, all that wealth e'er gave,
Await alike th' inevitable hour.
    The paths of glory lead but to the grave.

Nor you, ye proud, impute to these the fault,
    If memory o'er their tomb no trophies raise,
Where through the long-drawn aisle and fretted vault,
    The pealing anthem swells the note of praise.

Can storied urn, or animated bust,
    Back to its mansion call the fleeting breath?
Can honour's voice provoke the silent dust,
    Or flatt'ry soothe the dull cold ear of death?

spot is laid.

Full many a flower is born to blush unseen.

Perhaps in this neglected spot is laid
   Some heart once pregnant with celestial fire;
Hands, that the rod of empire might have sway'd,
   Or waked to ecstasy the living lyre:

But Knowledge to their eyes her ample page
   Rich with the spoils of time did ne'er unroll;
Chill Penury repress'd their noble rage,
   And froze the genial current of the soul.

Full many a gem of purest ray serene
   The dark unfathom'd caves of ocean bear:
Full many a flower is born to blush unseen,
   And waste its sweetness on the desert air.

9

Some village Hampden, that, with dauntless breast.

Some village Hampden, that, with dauntless breast,
    The little tyrant of his fields withstood,
Some mute inglorious Milton here may rest,
    Some Cromwell guiltless of his country's blood.

Th' applause of list'ning senates to command,
    The threats of pain and ruin to despise,
To scatter plenty o'er a smiling land,
    And read their history in a nation's eyes.

Their lot forbade : nor circumscribed alone
    Their growing virtues, but their crimes confined
Forbade to wade thro' slaughter to a throne,
    And shut the gates of mercy on mankind,

Along the cool sequestered vale of life.

The struggling pangs of conscious truth to hide,
  To quench the blushes of ingenuous shame,
Or heap the shrine of luxury and pride
  With incense kindled at the Muse's flame.

Far from the madding crowd's ignoble strife,
  Their sober wishes never learn'd to stray ;
Along the cool sequester'd vale of life
  They kept the noiseless tenor of their way.

Yet e'en these bones from insult to protect
  Some frail memorial still erected nigh,
With uncouth rhymes and shapeless sculpture deck'd,
  Implores the passing tribute of a sigh.

11

On some fond breast the parting soul relies.

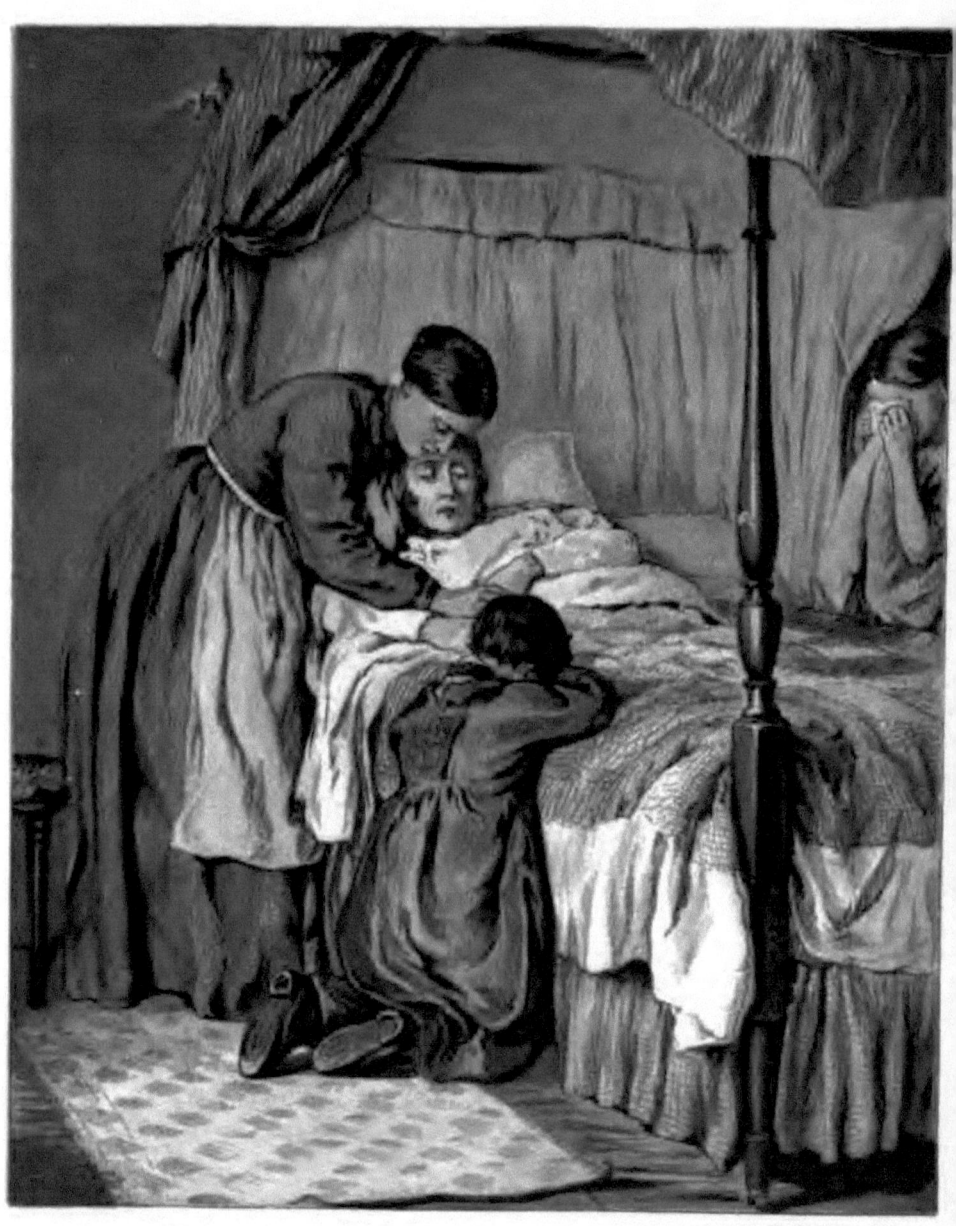

Their name, their years, spelt by th' unletter'd Muse,
The place of fame and elegy supply :
And many a holy text around she strews,
That teach the rustic moralist to die.

For who, to dumb forgetfulness a prey,
This pleasing anxious being e'er resign'd,
Left the warm precincts of the cheerful day,
Nor cast one longing ling'ring look behind ?

On some fond breast the parting soul relies,
Some pious drops the closing eye requires ;
E'en from the tomb the voice of nature cries,
E'en in our ashes live their wonted fires.

12

There at the foot of yonder nodding beech.

For thee, who, mindful of th' unhonour'd Dead,
　Dost in these lines their artless tale relate ;
If chance, by lonely contemplation led,
　Some kindred spirit shall enquire thy fate,—

Haply some hoary-headed swain may say,
　"Oft have we seen him at the peep of dawn,
Brushing with hasty steps the dews away,
　To meet the sun upon the upland lawn :

"There at the foot of yonder nodding beech,
　That wreathes its old fantastic roots so high,
His listless length at noontide would he stretch,
　And pore upon the brook that babbles by.

Slow through the church-way path we saw it borne.

"Hard by yon wood, now smiling as in scorn,
　Mutt'ring his wayward fancies he would rove;
Now drooping, woful-wan, like one forlorn,
　Or crazed with care, or cross'd in hopeless love.

"One morn I miss'd him on th' accustom'd hill,
　Along the heath, and near his fav'rite tree;
Another came; nor yet beside the rill,
　Nor up the lawn, nor at the wood was ·he:

"The next, with dirges due in sad array,
　Slow through the church-way path we saw him borne;
Approach and read (for thou canst read) the lay
　Grav'd on the stone beneath yon aged thorn."

14

The Epitaph.

Here rests his head upon the lap of earth
  A youth, to fortune and to fame unknown:
Fair Science frown'd not on his humble birth,
  And Melancholy mark'd him for her own.

Large was his bounty, and his soul sincere,
  Heaven did a recompense as largely send:
He gave to misery (all he had) a tear,
  He gain'd from heaven ('twas all he wish'd) a friend.

No farther seek his merits to disclose,
  Or draw his frailties from their dread abode,
(There they alike in trembling hope repose,)
  The bosom of his Father and his God.

15

The manuscript from which the present Facsimile has been taken, is the only existing draught of the Poem, the Autograph at Pembroke House, Cambridge, being manifestly a fair copy made by the Poet, probably for circulation among his friends. This draught formed a portion of the papers bequeathed by Gray to his friend and biographer, Mason.